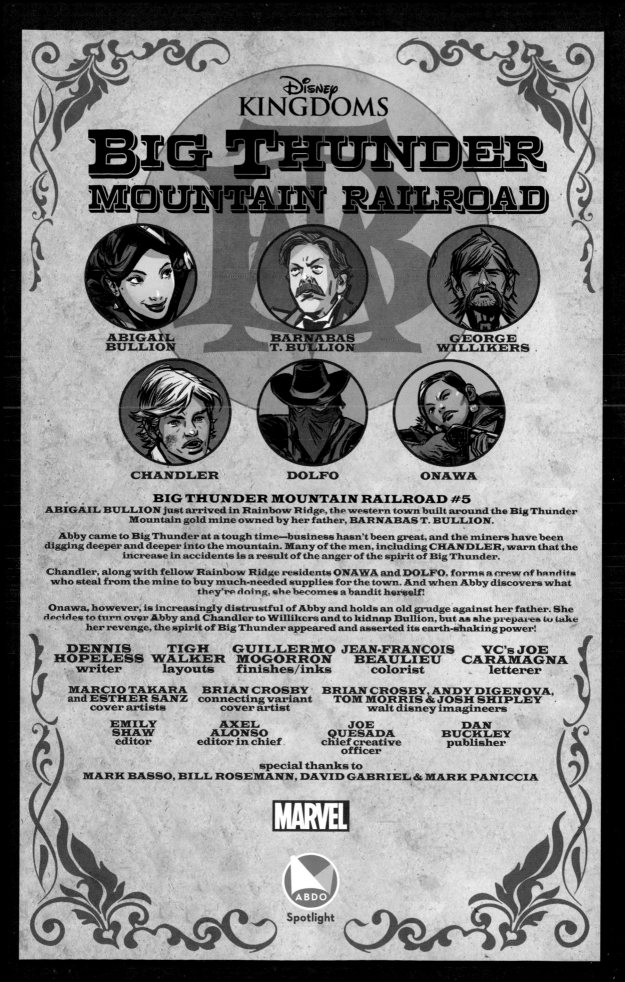

DISNEY KINGDOMS

BIG THUNDER
MOUNTAIN RAILROAD

ABIGAIL BULLION

BARNABAS T. BULLION

GEORGE WILLIKERS

CHANDLER

DOLFO

ONAWA

BIG THUNDER MOUNTAIN RAILROAD #5

ABIGAIL BULLION just arrived in Rainbow Ridge, the western town built around the Big Thunder Mountain gold mine owned by her father, **BARNABAS T. BULLION.**

Abby came to Big Thunder at a tough time—business hasn't been great, and the miners have been digging deeper and deeper into the mountain. Many of the men, including **CHANDLER,** warn that the increase in accidents is a result of the anger of the spirit of Big Thunder.

Chandler, along with fellow Rainbow Ridge residents **ONAWA** and **DOLFO,** forms a crew of bandits who steal from the mine to buy much-needed supplies for the town. And when Abby discovers what they're doing, she becomes a bandit herself!

Onawa, however, is increasingly distrustful of Abby and holds an old grudge against her father. She decides to turn over Abby and Chandler to Willikers and to kidnap Bullion, but as she prepares to take her revenge, the spirit of Big Thunder appeared and asserted its earth-shaking power!

DENNIS HOPELESS
writer

TIGH WALKER
layouts

GUILLERMO MOGORRON
finishes/inks

JEAN-FRANCOIS BEAULIEU
colorist

VC's JOE CARAMAGNA
letterer

MARCIO TAKARA and **ESTHER SANZ**
cover artists

BRIAN CROSBY
connecting variant cover artist

BRIAN CROSBY, ANDY DIGENOVA, TOM MORRIS & JOSH SHIPLEY
walt disney imagineers

EMILY SHAW
editor

AXEL ALONSO
editor in chief

JOE QUESADA
chief creative officer

DAN BUCKLEY
publisher

special thanks to
MARK BASSO, BILL ROSEMANN, DAVID GABRIEL & MARK PANICCIA

MARVEL

ABDO
Spotlight

ABDOPUBLISHING.COM

Reinforced library bound edition published in 2017 by Spotlight,
a division of ABDO, PO Box 398166, Minneapolis, Minnesota 55439.
Spotlight produces high-quality reinforced library bound editions for
schools and libraries. Published by agreement with Marvel Characters, Inc.

Printed in the United States of America, North Mankato, Minnesota.
092016
012017

THIS BOOK CONTAINS
RECYCLED MATERIALS

marvelkids.com

© 2015 MARVEL

**Elements based on Walt Disney's
Big Thunder Mountain Railroad © Disney.**

PUBLISHER'S CATALOGING IN PUBLICATION DATA

Names: Hopeless, Dennis, author. | Walker, Tigh ; Beaulieu, Jean-Francois ; Ruiz, Felix ;
   Mogorron, Guillermo, illustrators.
Title: Big Thunder Mountain Railroad / writer: Dennis Hopeless ; art: Tigh Walker ;
   Jean-Francois Beaulieu ; Felix Ruiz ; Guillermo Mogorron.
Description: Reinforced library bound edition. | Minneapolis, Minnesota : Spotlight, 2017. |
   Series: Disney Kingdoms: Big Thunder Mountain Railroad | Volumes 1, 2 and 4 written by
   Dennis Hopeless ; illustrated by Tigh Walker & Jean-Francois Beaulieu. | Volume 3 written
   by Dennis Hopeless ; illustrated by Felix Ruiz & Jean-Francois Beaulieu. | Volume 5 written
   by Dennis Hopeless ; illustrated by Tigh Walker, Guillermo Mogorron & Jean-Francois
   Beaulieu.
Summary: When Abby traveled west to Rainbow Ridge to live with her father Barnabas T.
   Bullion at the Big Thunder Mountain gold mine, the brave young hero never thought
   she'd join a group of bandits to rob her own father's mine.
Identifiers: LCCN 2016941684 | ISBN 9781614795759 (v.1 ; lib. bdg.) | ISBN 9781614795766
   (v.2 ; lib. bdg.) | ISBN 9781614795773 (v.3 ; lib. bdg.) | ISBN 9781614795780 (v.4 ; lib.
   bdg.) | ISBN 9781614795797 (v.5 ; lib. bdg.)
Subjects: Disney (Fictitious characters)--Juvenile fiction. | Adventures and adventurers--Juvenile
   fiction. | Graphic novels--Juvenile fiction.
Classification: DDC 741.5--dc23
LC record available at https://lccn.loc.gov/2016941684

Spotlight

A Division of ABDO
abdopublishing.com

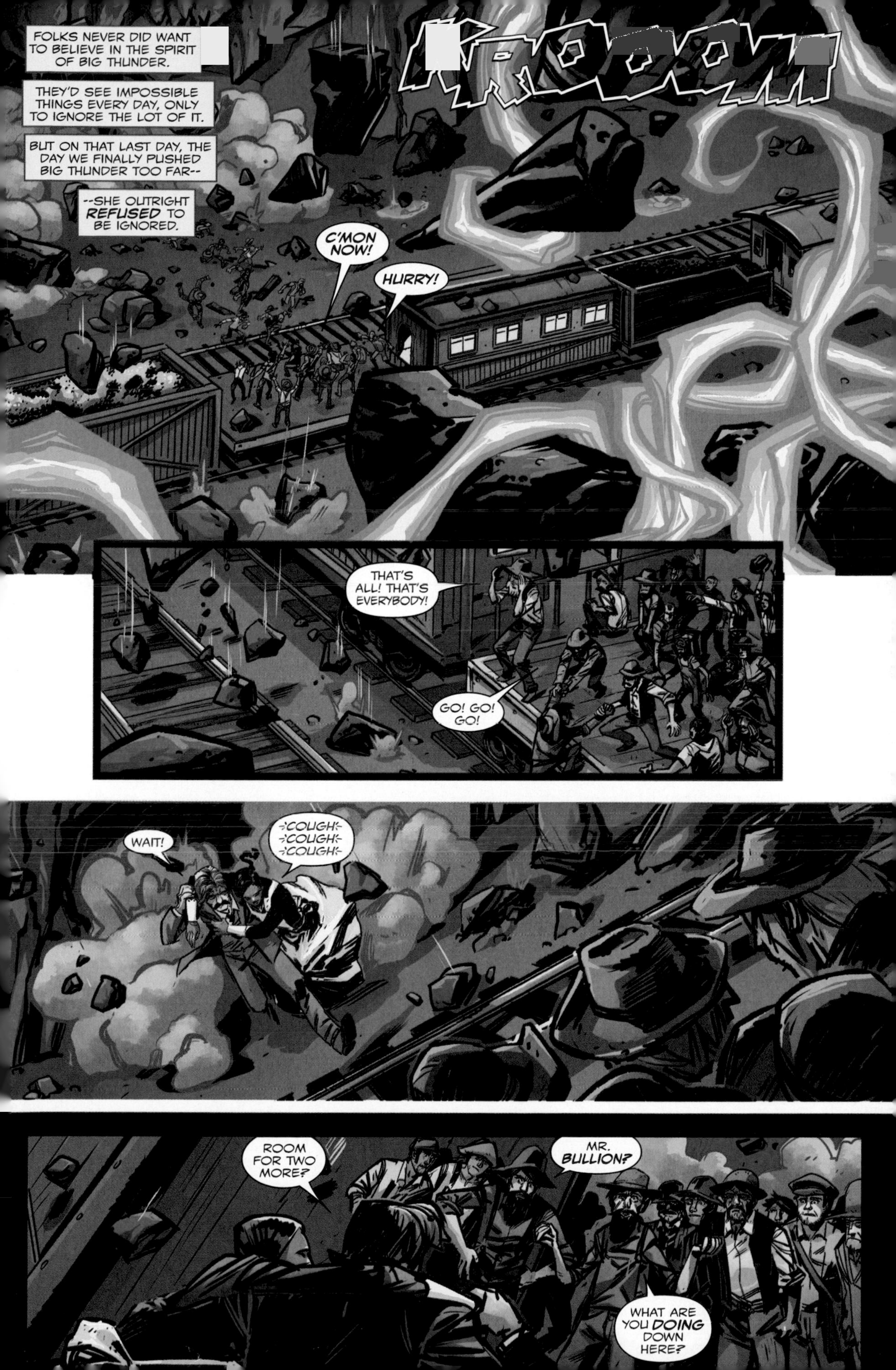
FOLKS NEVER DID WANT TO BELIEVE IN THE SPIRIT OF BIG THUNDER.
THEY'D SEE IMPOSSIBLE THINGS EVERY DAY, ONLY TO IGNORE THE LOT OF IT.
BUT ON THAT LAST DAY, THE DAY WE FINALLY PUSHED BIG THUNDER TOO FAR--
--SHE OUTRIGHT **REFUSED** TO BE IGNORED.
C'MON NOW!
HURRY!
THAT'S ALL! THAT'S EVERYBODY!
GO! GO! GO!
WAIT!
COUGH COUGH COUGH
ROOM FOR TWO MORE?
MR. **BULLION?**
WHAT ARE YOU **DOING** DOWN HERE?

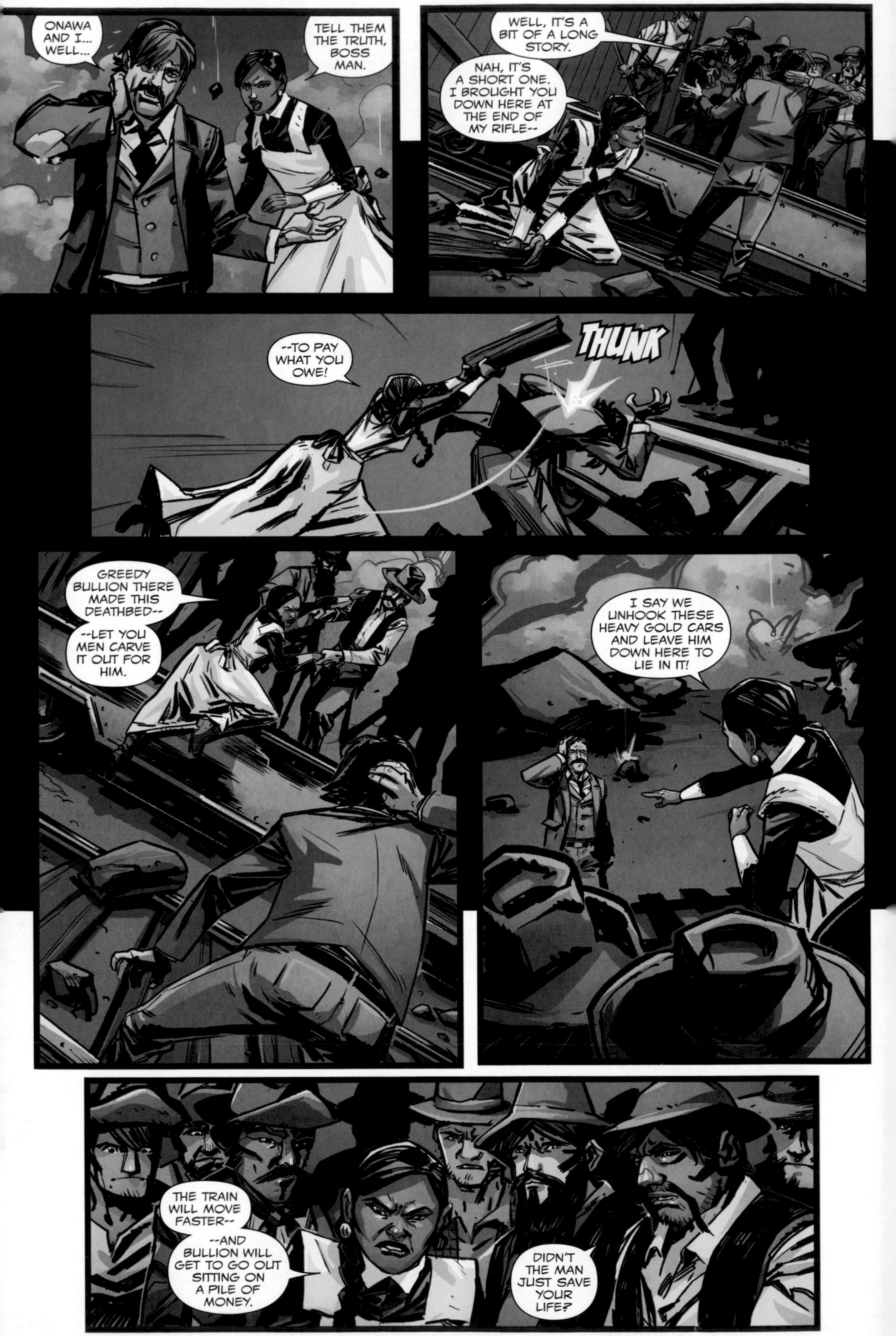
ONAWA AND I... WELL...
TELL THEM THE TRUTH, BOSS MAN.
WELL, IT'S A BIT OF A LONG STORY.
NAH, IT'S A SHORT ONE. I BROUGHT YOU DOWN HERE AT THE END OF MY RIFLE--
--TO PAY WHAT YOU OWE!
THUNK
GREEDY BULLION THERE MADE THIS DEATHBED--
--LET YOU MEN CARVE IT OUT FOR HIM.
I SAY WE UNHOOK THESE HEAVY GOLD CARS AND LEAVE HIM DOWN HERE TO LIE IN IT!
THE TRAIN WILL MOVE FASTER--
--AND BULLION WILL GET TO GO OUT SITTING ON A PILE OF MONEY.
DIDN'T THE MAN JUST SAVE YOUR LIFE?

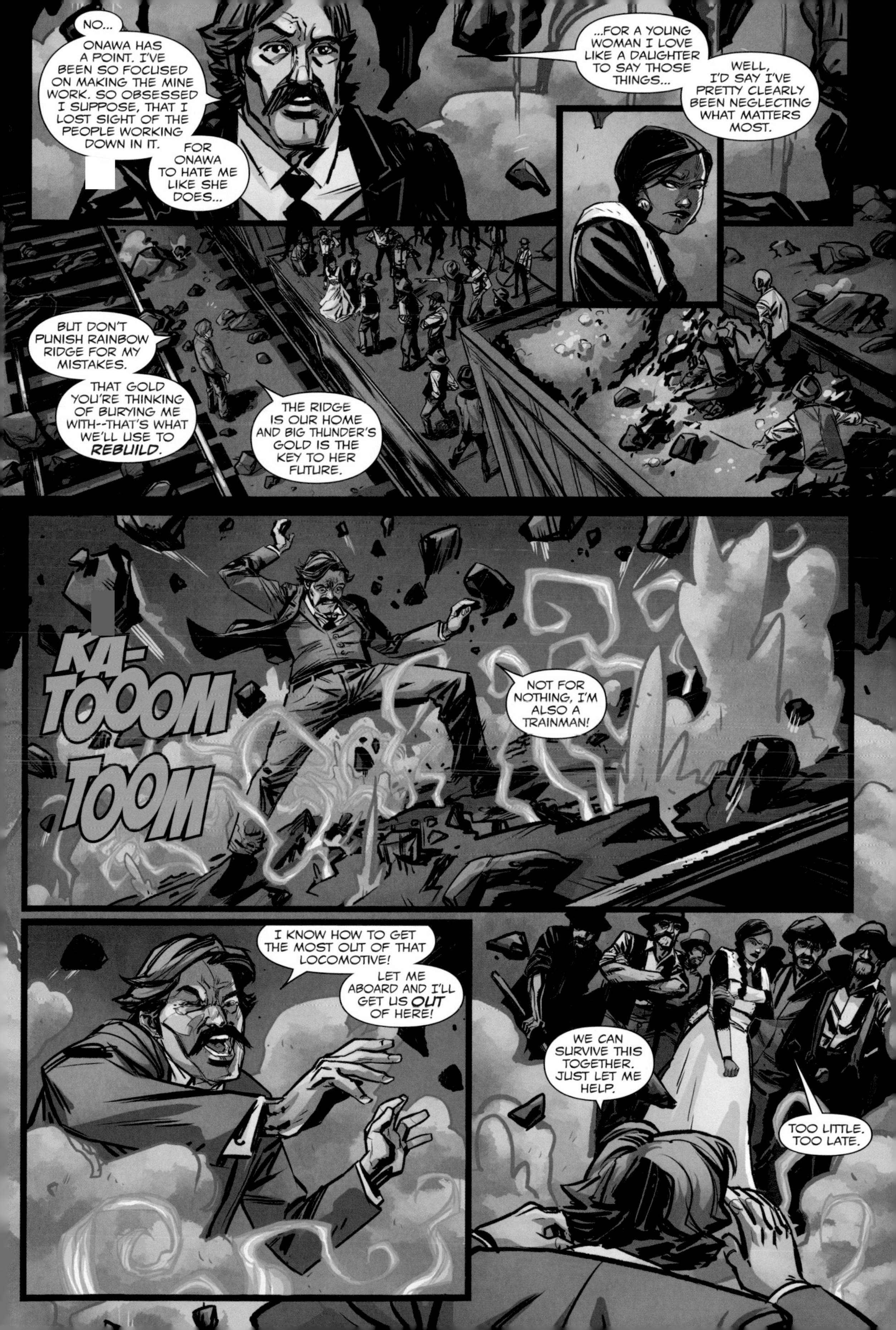

NO...
ONAWA HAS A POINT. I'VE BEEN SO FOCUSED ON MAKING THE MINE WORK. SO OBSESSED I SUPPOSE, THAT I LOST SIGHT OF THE PEOPLE WORKING DOWN IN IT.
FOR ONAWA TO HATE ME LIKE SHE DOES...
...FOR A YOUNG WOMAN I LOVE LIKE A DAUGHTER TO SAY THOSE THINGS...
WELL, I'D SAY I'VE PRETTY CLEARLY BEEN NEGLECTING WHAT MATTERS MOST.
BUT DON'T PUNISH RAINBOW RIDGE FOR MY MISTAKES.
THAT GOLD YOU'RE THINKING OF BURYING ME WITH--THAT'S WHAT WE'LL USE TO REBUILD.
THE RIDGE IS OUR HOME AND BIG THUNDER'S GOLD IS THE KEY TO HER FUTURE.
KA-TOOOM TOOM
NOT FOR NOTHING, I'M ALSO A TRAINMAN!
I KNOW HOW TO GET THE MOST OUT OF THAT LOCOMOTIVE!
LET ME ABOARD AND I'LL GET US OUT OF HERE!
WE CAN SURVIVE THIS TOGETHER. JUST LET ME HELP.
TOO LITTLE. TOO LATE.

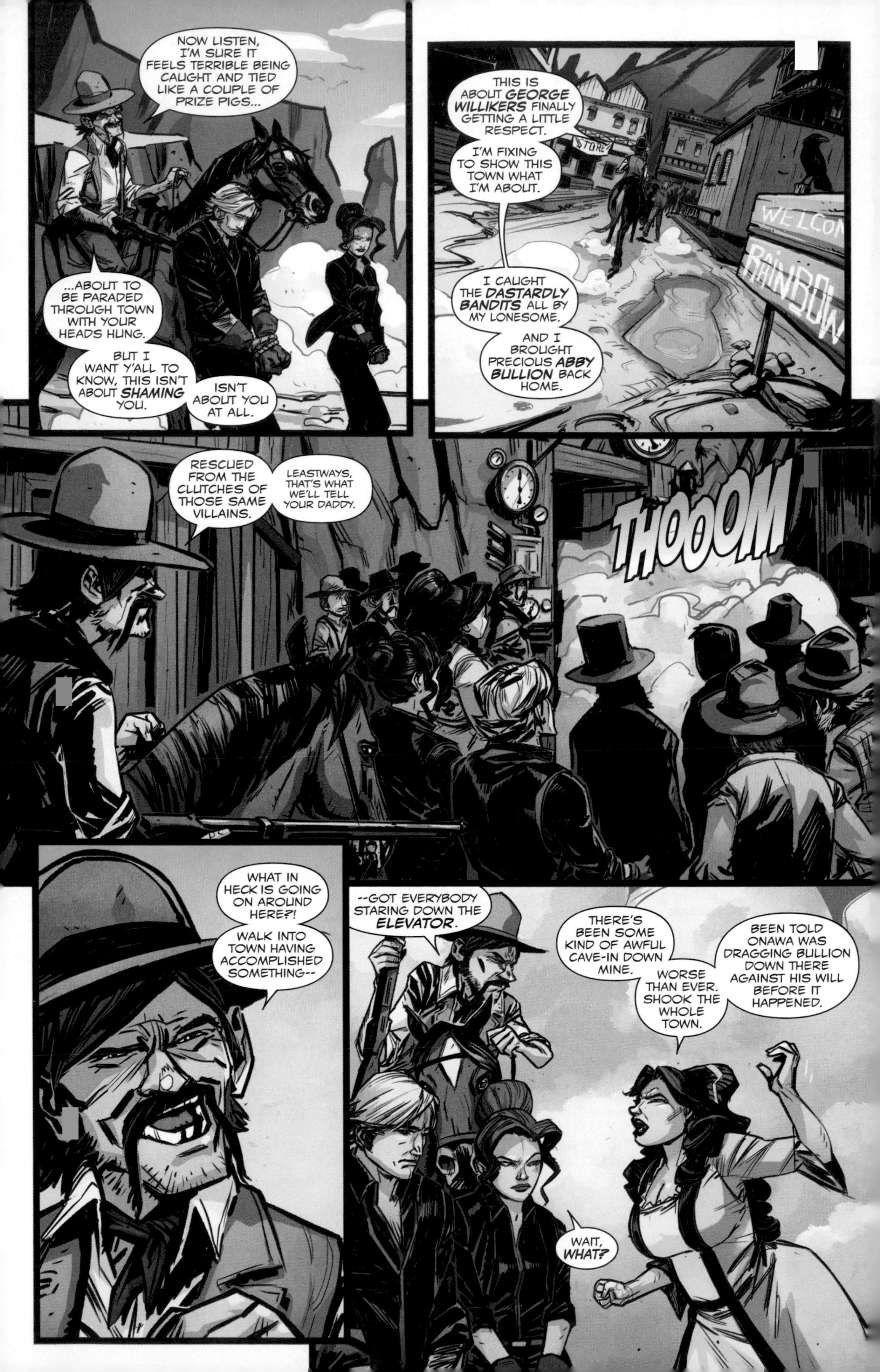
NOW LISTEN, I'M SURE IT FEELS TERRIBLE BEING CAUGHT AND TIED LIKE A COUPLE OF PRIZE PIGS...
...ABOUT TO BE PARADED THROUGH TOWN WITH YOUR HEADS HUNG.
BUT I WANT Y'ALL TO KNOW, THIS ISN'T ABOUT SHAMING YOU.
ISN'T ABOUT YOU AT ALL.
THIS IS ABOUT GEORGE WILLIKERS FINALLY GETTING A LITTLE RESPECT.
I'M FIXING TO SHOW THIS TOWN WHAT I'M ABOUT.
STORE
WELCOM
RAINBOW
I CAUGHT THE DASTARDLY BANDITS ALL BY MY LONESOME.
AND I BROUGHT PRECIOUS ABBY BULLION BACK HOME.
RESCUED FROM THE CLUTCHES OF THOSE SAME VILLAINS.
LEASTWAYS, THAT'S WHAT WE'LL TELL YOUR DADDY.
THOOOM
WHAT IN HECK IS GOING ON AROUND HERE?!
WALK INTO TOWN HAVING ACCOMPLISHED SOMETHING--
--GOT EVERYBODY STARING DOWN THE ELEVATOR.
THERE'S BEEN SOME KIND OF AWFUL CAVE-IN DOWN MINE.
WORSE THAN EVER. SHOOK THE WHOLE TOWN.
BEEN TOLD ONAWA WAS DRAGGING BULLION DOWN THERE AGAINST HIS WILL BEFORE IT HAPPENED.
WAIT, WHAT?

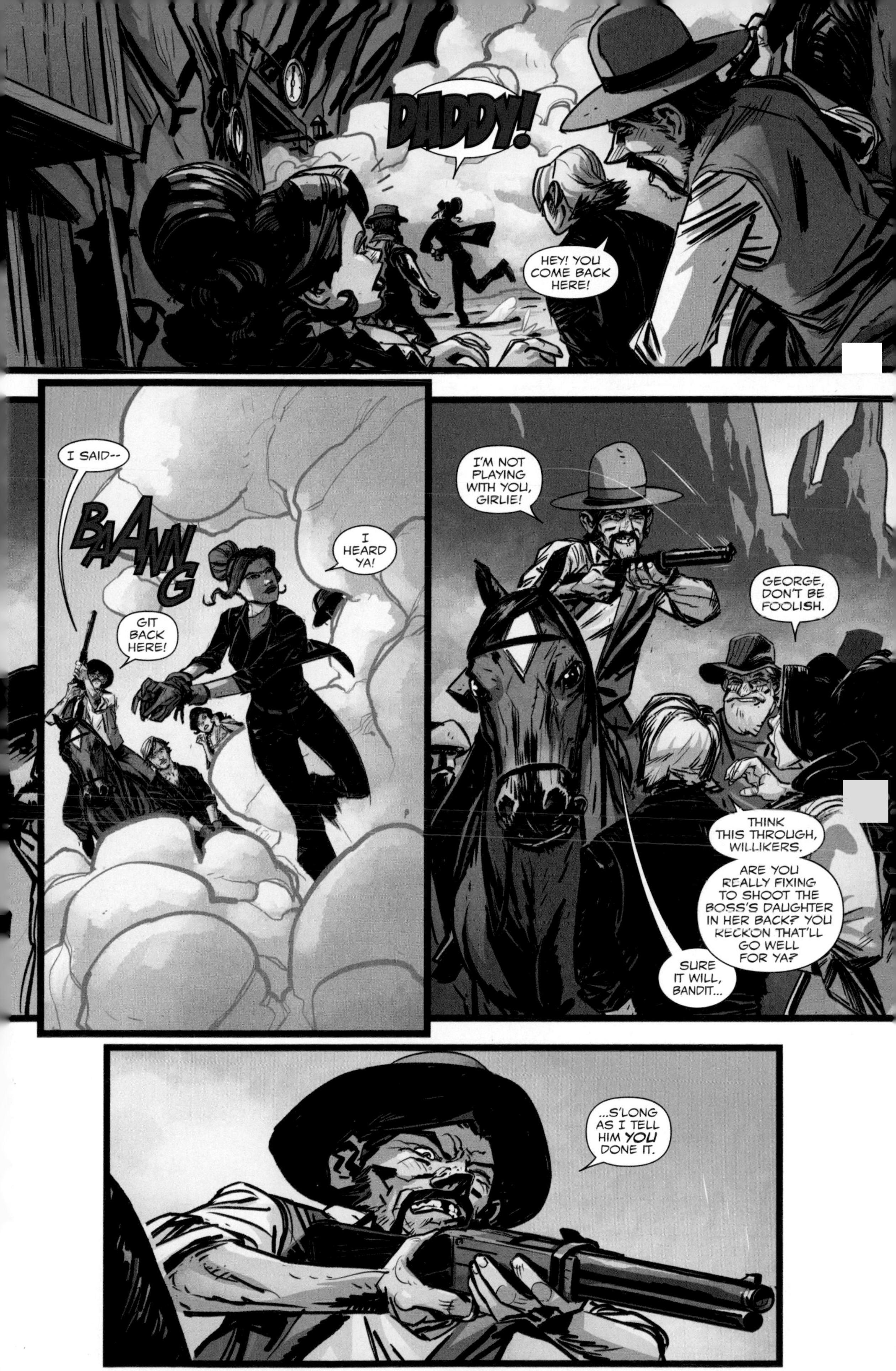
DADDY!
HEY! YOU COME BACK HERE!
I SAID--
BAANNG
I HEARD YA!
GIT BACK HERE!
I'M NOT PLAYING WITH YOU, GIRLIE!
GEORGE, DON'T BE FOOLISH.
THINK THIS THROUGH, WILLIKERS.
ARE YOU REALLY FIXING TO SHOOT THE BOSS'S DAUGHTER IN HER BACK? YOU RECKON THAT'LL GO WELL FOR YA?
SURE IT WILL, BANDIT...
...S'LONG AS I TELL HIM *YOU* DONE IT.

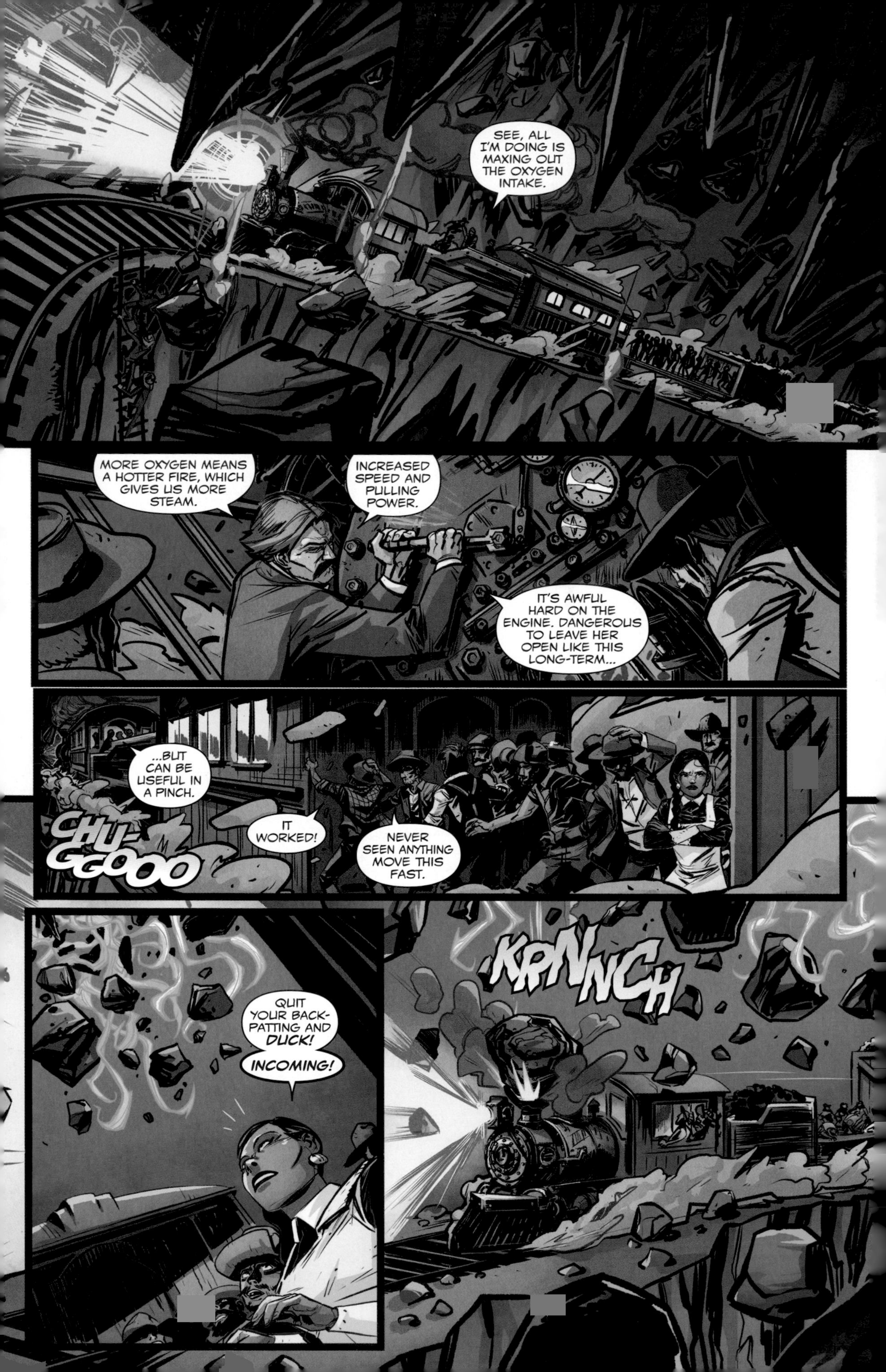
SEE, ALL I'M DOING IS MAXING OUT THE OXYGEN INTAKE.
MORE OXYGEN MEANS A HOTTER FIRE, WHICH GIVES US MORE STEAM.
INCREASED SPEED AND PULLING POWER.
IT'S AWFUL HARD ON THE ENGINE. DANGEROUS TO LEAVE HER OPEN LIKE THIS LONG-TERM...
...BUT CAN BE USEFUL IN A PINCH.
CHU-GGOOO
IT WORKED!
NEVER SEEN ANYTHING MOVE THIS FAST.
QUIT YOUR BACK-PATTING AND DUCK!
INCOMING!
KRNNCH

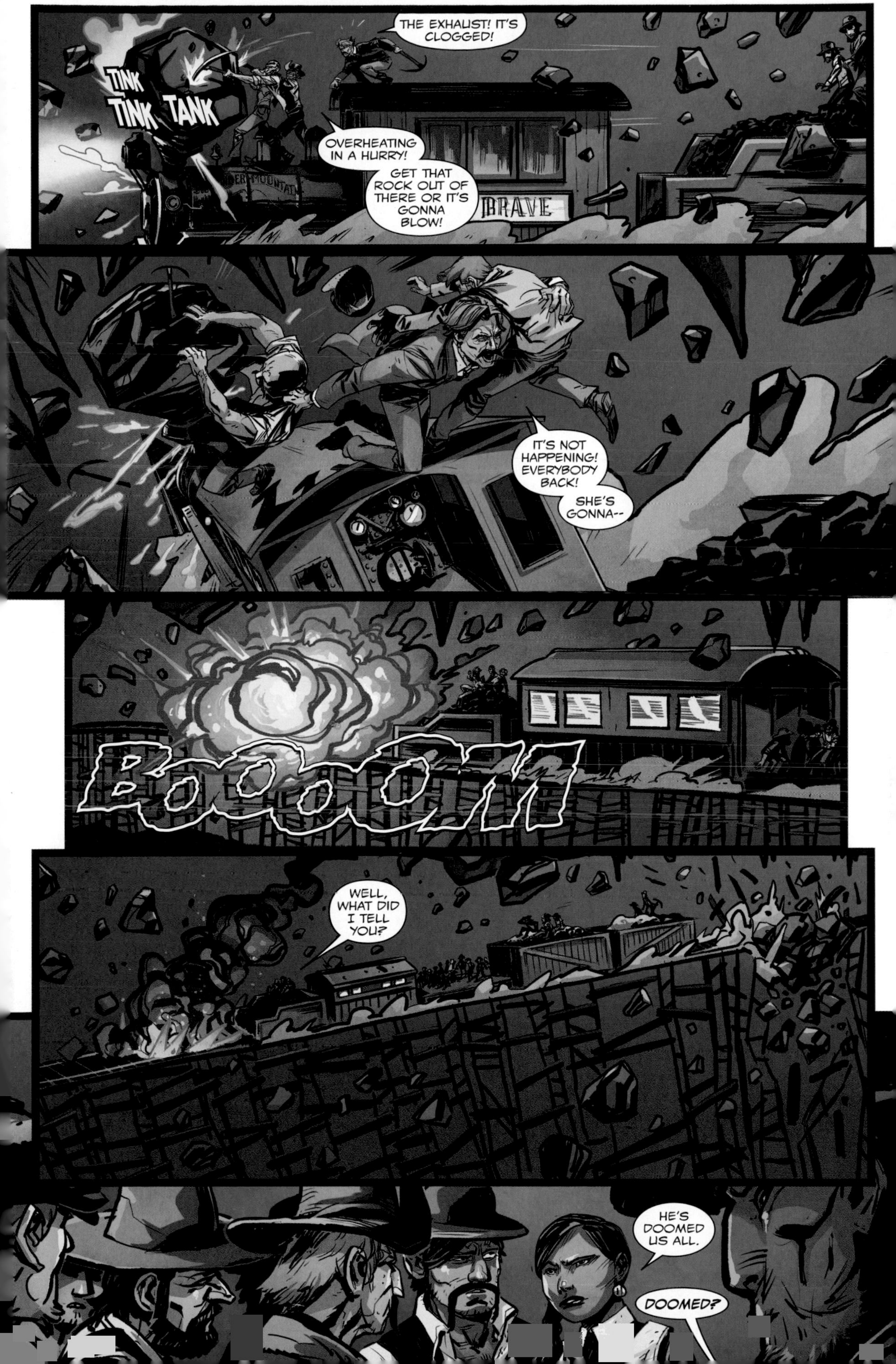
TINK
TINK TANK
THE EXHAUST! IT'S CLOGGED!
OVERHEATING IN A HURRY!
GET THAT ROCK OUT OF THERE OR IT'S GONNA BLOW!
BRAVE
IT'S NOT HAPPENING! EVERYBODY BACK!
SHE'S GONNA--
BOOOOM
WELL, WHAT DID I TELL YOU?
HE'S DOOMED US ALL.
DOOMED?

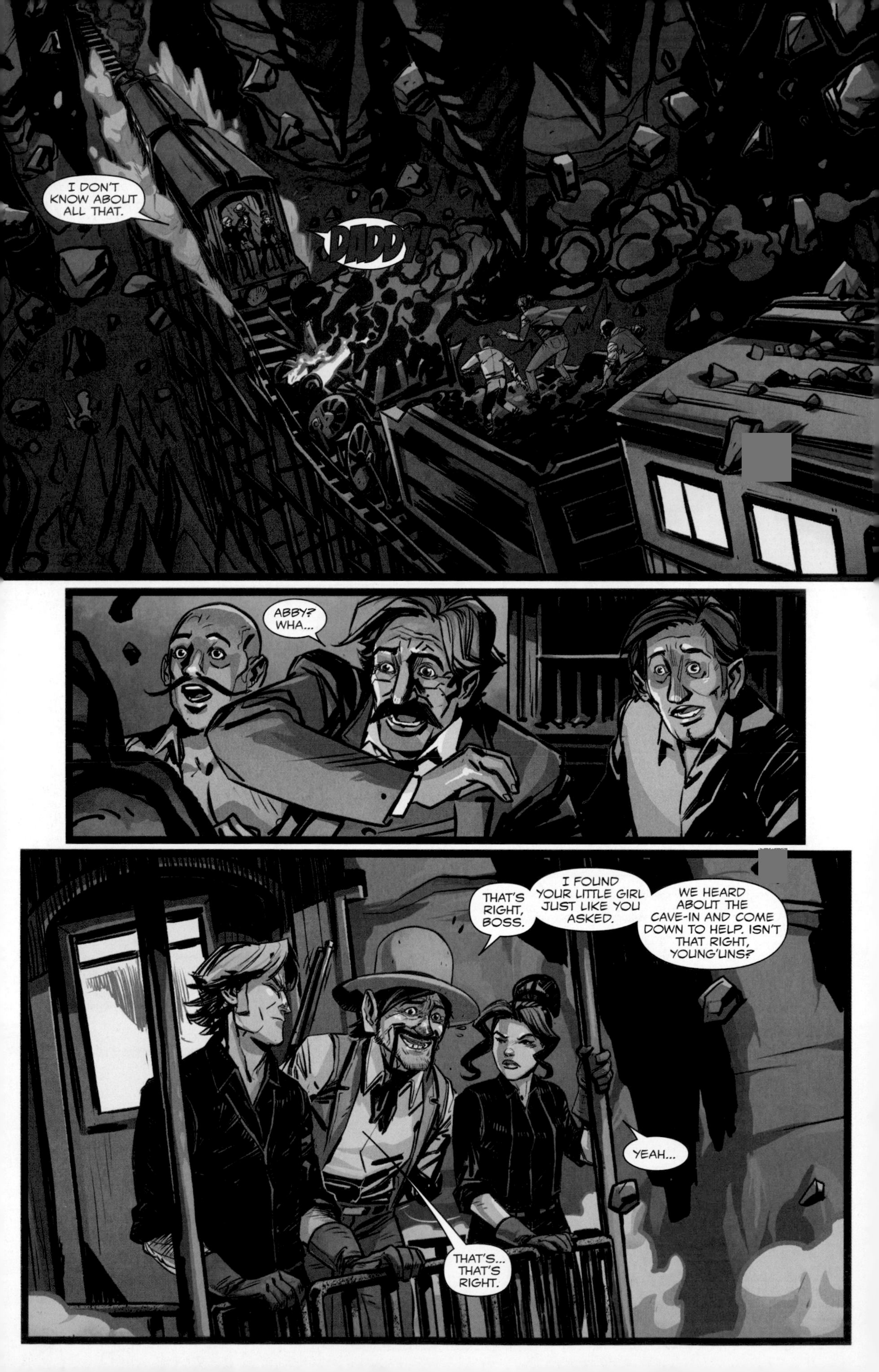
I DON'T KNOW ABOUT ALL THAT.
DADDY!
ABBY? WHA...
THAT'S RIGHT, BOSS.
I FOUND YOUR LITTLE GIRL JUST LIKE YOU ASKED.
WE HEARD ABOUT THE CAVE-IN AND COME DOWN TO HELP. ISN'T THAT RIGHT, YOUNG'UNS?
YEAH...
THAT'S... THAT'S RIGHT.

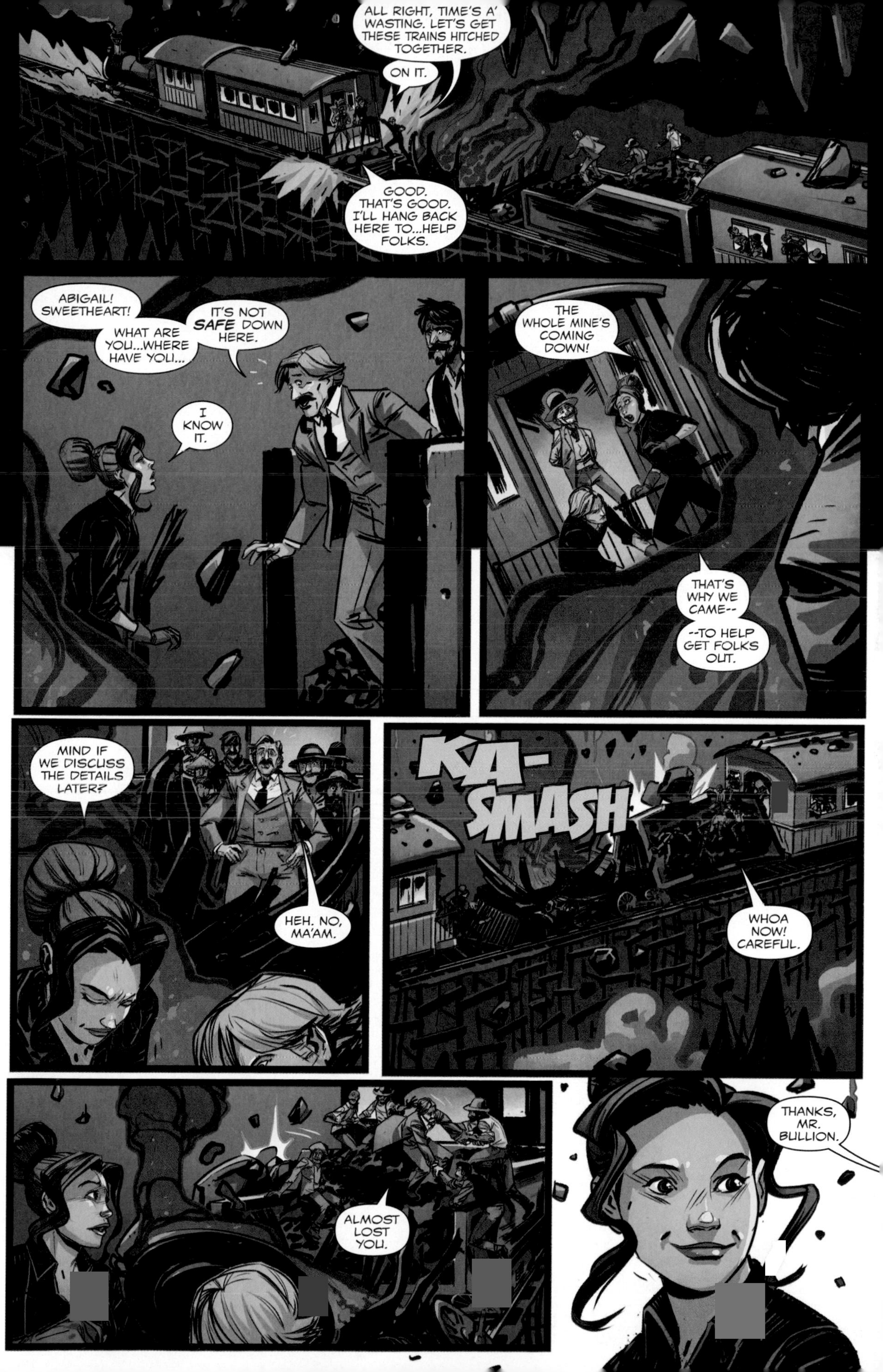
ALL RIGHT, TIME'S A' WASTING. LET'S GET THESE TRAINS HITCHED TOGETHER.
ON IT.
GOOD. THAT'S GOOD. I'LL HANG BACK HERE TO...HELP FOLKS.
ABIGAIL! SWEETHEART!
WHAT ARE YOU...WHERE HAVE YOU...
IT'S NOT SAFE DOWN HERE.
I KNOW IT.
THE WHOLE MINE'S COMING DOWN!
THAT'S WHY WE CAME--
--TO HELP GET FOLKS OUT.
MIND IF WE DISCUSS THE DETAILS LATER?
HEH. NO, MA'AM.
KA-SMASH
WHOA NOW! CAREFUL.
ALMOST LOST YOU.
THANKS, MR. BULLION.

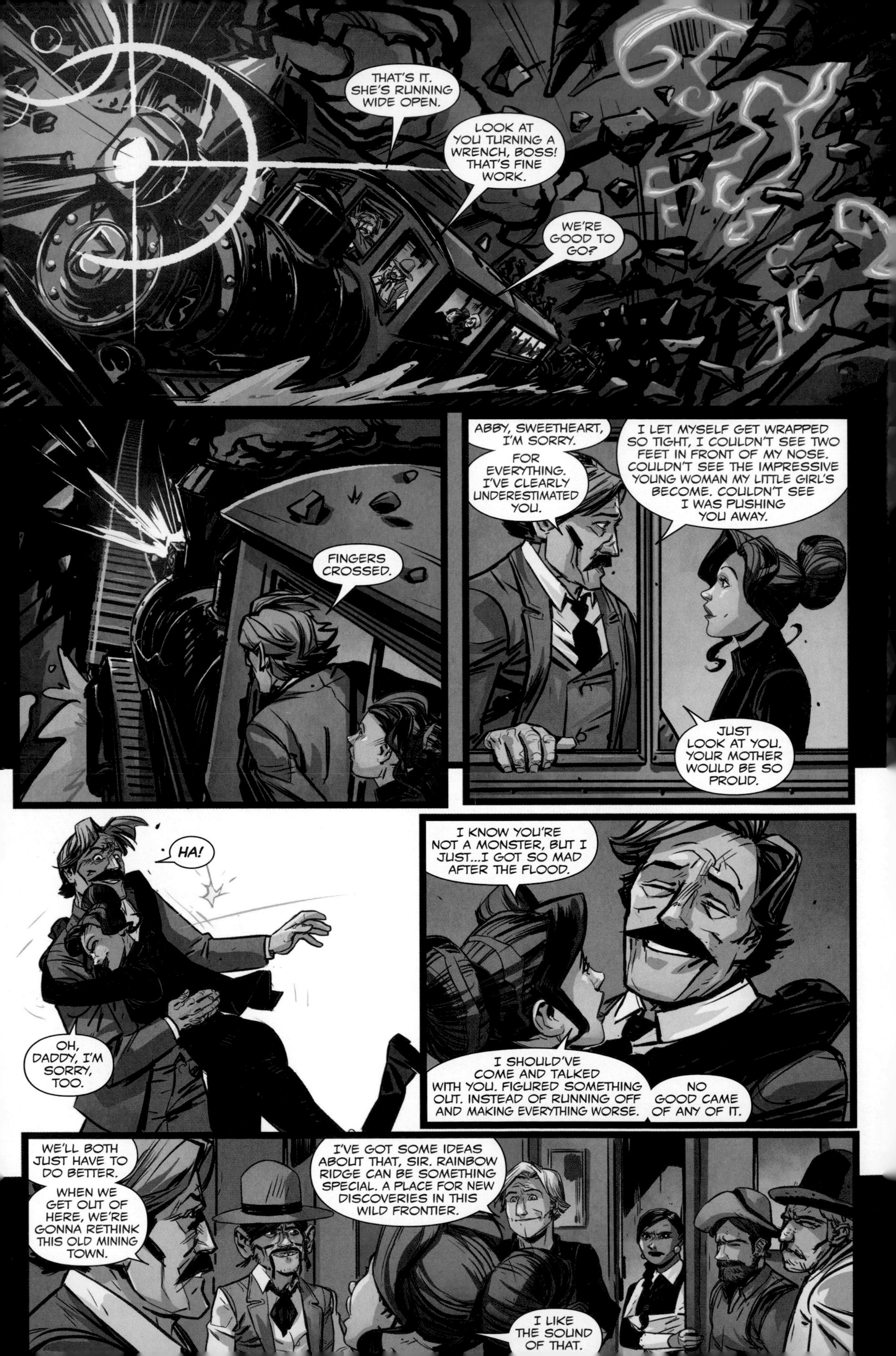
THAT'S IT. SHE'S RUNNING WIDE OPEN.
LOOK AT YOU TURNING A WRENCH, BOSS! THAT'S FINE WORK.
WE'RE GOOD TO GO?
FINGERS CROSSED.
ABBY, SWEETHEART, I'M SORRY.
FOR EVERYTHING. I'VE CLEARLY UNDERESTIMATED YOU.
I LET MYSELF GET WRAPPED SO TIGHT, I COULDN'T SEE TWO FEET IN FRONT OF MY NOSE. COULDN'T SEE THE IMPRESSIVE YOUNG WOMAN MY LITTLE GIRL'S BECOME. COULDN'T SEE I WAS PUSHING YOU AWAY.
JUST LOOK AT YOU. YOUR MOTHER WOULD BE SO PROUD.
HA!
OH, DADDY, I'M SORRY, TOO.
I KNOW YOU'RE NOT A MONSTER, BUT I JUST...I GOT SO MAD AFTER THE FLOOD.
I SHOULD'VE COME AND TALKED WITH YOU. FIGURED SOMETHING OUT. INSTEAD OF RUNNING OFF AND MAKING EVERYTHING WORSE.
NO GOOD CAME OF ANY OF IT.
WE'LL BOTH JUST HAVE TO DO BETTER.
WHEN WE GET OUT OF HERE, WE'RE GONNA RETHINK THIS OLD MINING TOWN.
I'VE GOT SOME IDEAS ABOUT THAT, SIR. RAINBOW RIDGE CAN BE SOMETHING SPECIAL. A PLACE FOR NEW DISCOVERIES IN THIS WILD FRONTIER.
I LIKE THE SOUND OF THAT.

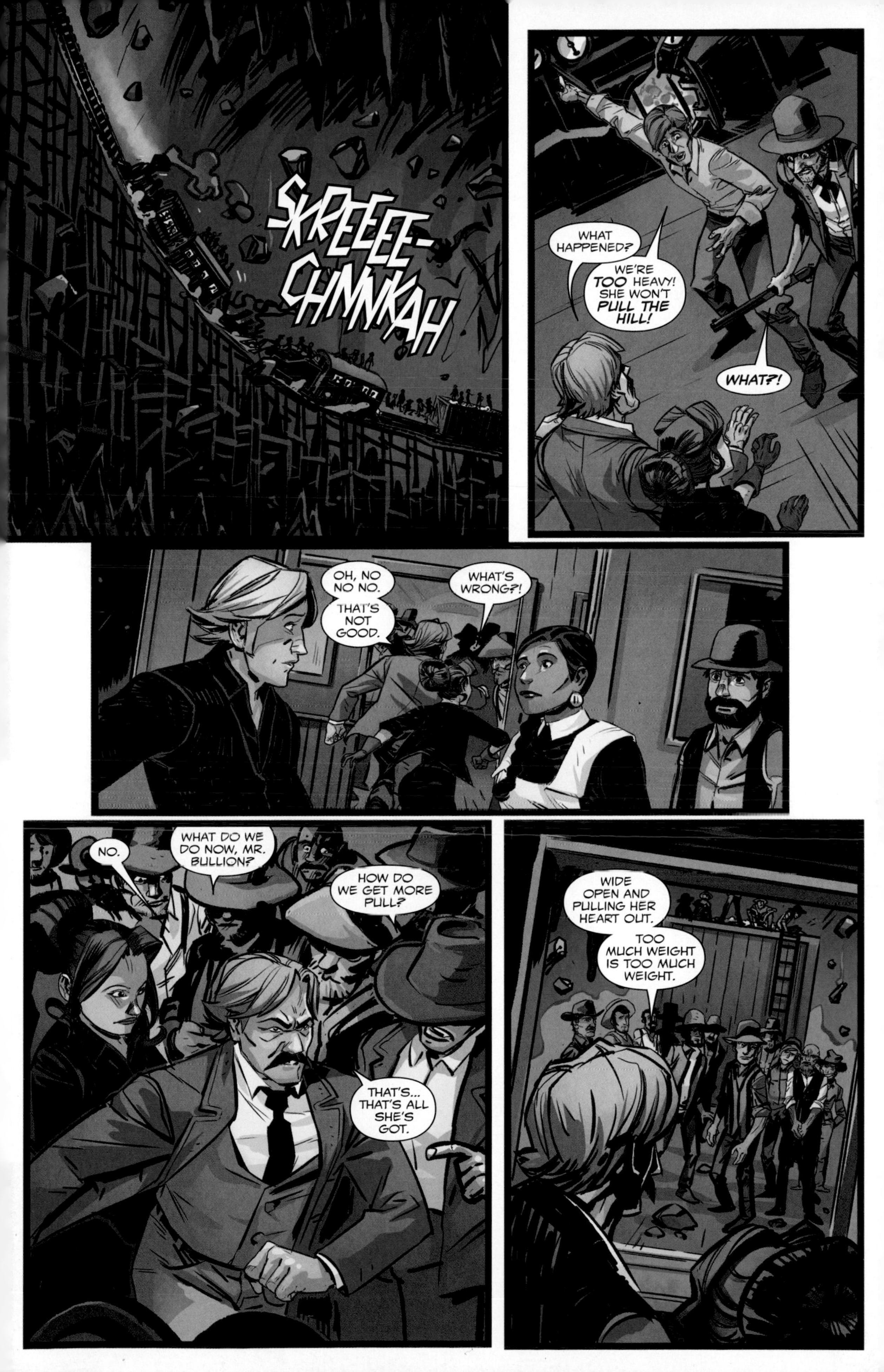
SKREEEE-
CHNNKAH
WHAT HAPPENED?
WE'RE TOO HEAVY! SHE WON'T PULL THE HILL!
WHAT?!
OH, NO NO NO.
THAT'S NOT GOOD.
WHAT'S WRONG?!
NO.
WHAT DO WE DO NOW, MR. BULLION?
HOW DO WE GET MORE PULL?
THAT'S... THAT'S ALL SHE'S GOT.
WIDE OPEN AND PULLING HER HEART OUT.
TOO MUCH WEIGHT IS TOO MUCH WEIGHT.

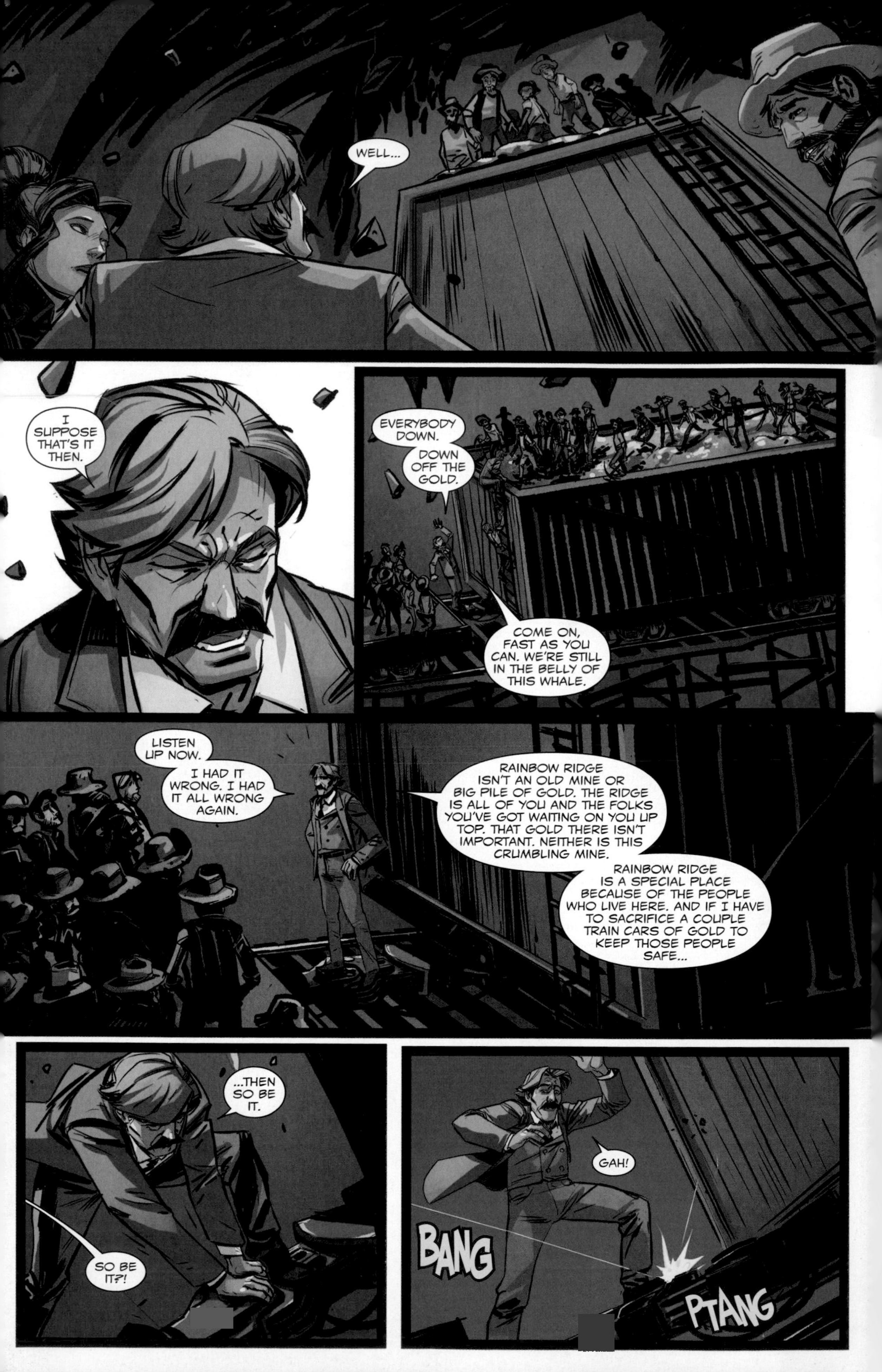
WELL...
I SUPPOSE THAT'S IT THEN.
EVERYBODY DOWN.
DOWN OFF THE GOLD.
COME ON, FAST AS YOU CAN. WE'RE STILL IN THE BELLY OF THIS WHALE.
LISTEN UP NOW.
I HAD IT WRONG. I HAD IT ALL WRONG AGAIN.
RAINBOW RIDGE ISN'T AN OLD MINE OR BIG PILE OF GOLD. THE RIDGE IS ALL OF YOU AND THE FOLKS YOU'VE GOT WAITING ON YOU UP TOP. THAT GOLD THERE ISN'T IMPORTANT. NEITHER IS THIS CRUMBLING MINE.
RAINBOW RIDGE IS A SPECIAL PLACE BECAUSE OF THE PEOPLE WHO LIVE HERE. AND IF I HAVE TO SACRIFICE A COUPLE TRAIN CARS OF GOLD TO KEEP THOSE PEOPLE SAFE...
...THEN SO BE IT.
SO BE IT?!
GAH!
BANG
PTANG

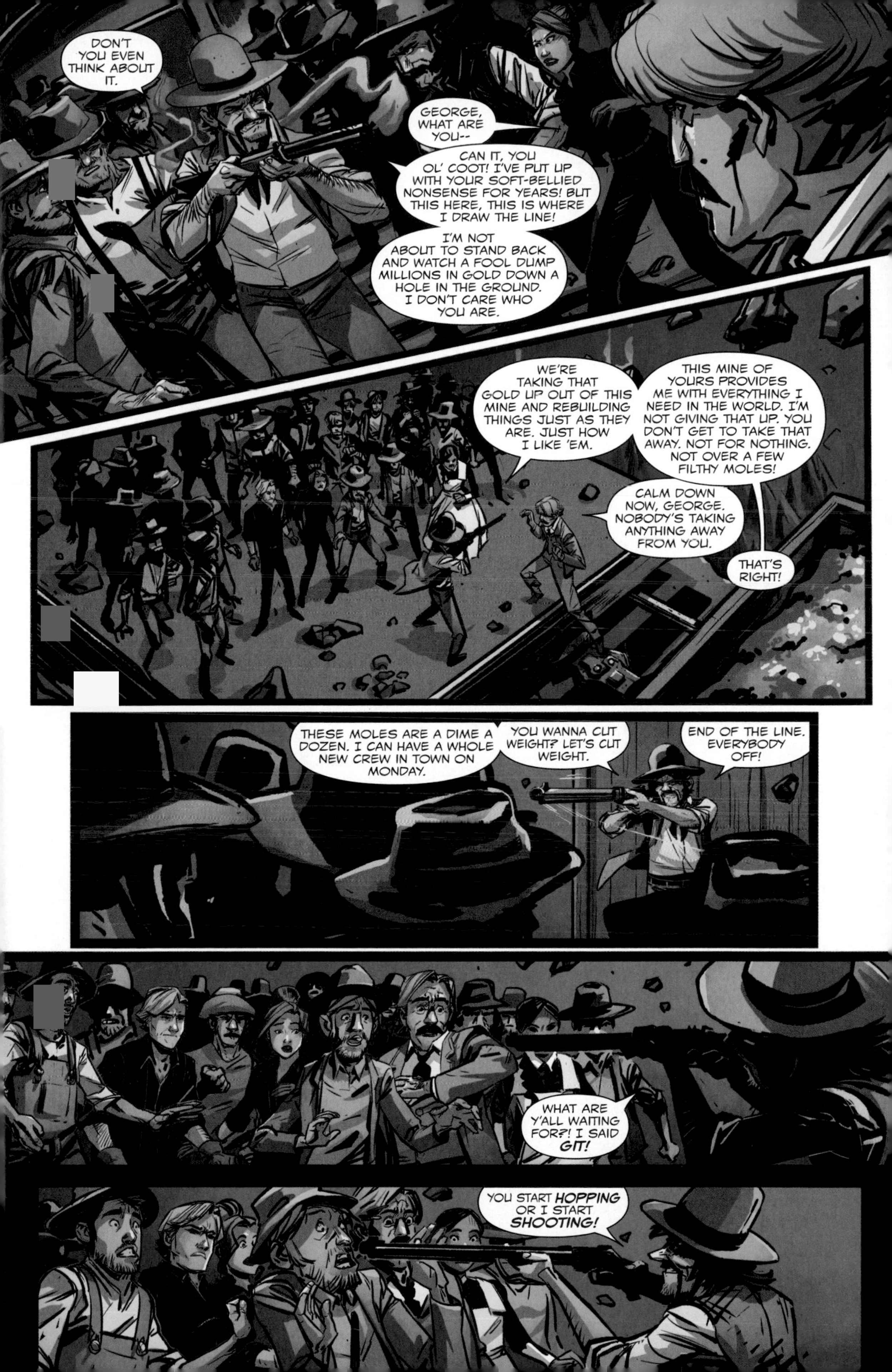
DON'T YOU EVEN THINK ABOUT IT.
GEORGE, WHAT ARE YOU--
CAN IT, YOU OL' COOT! I'VE PUT UP WITH YOUR SOFT-BELLIED NONSENSE FOR YEARS! BUT THIS HERE, THIS IS WHERE I DRAW THE LINE!
I'M NOT ABOUT TO STAND BACK AND WATCH A FOOL DUMP MILLIONS IN GOLD DOWN A HOLE IN THE GROUND. I DON'T CARE WHO YOU ARE.
WE'RE TAKING THAT GOLD UP OUT OF THIS MINE AND REBUILDING THINGS JUST AS THEY ARE. JUST HOW I LIKE 'EM.
THIS MINE OF YOURS PROVIDES ME WITH EVERYTHING I NEED IN THE WORLD. I'M NOT GIVING THAT UP. YOU DON'T GET TO TAKE THAT AWAY. NOT FOR NOTHING. NOT OVER A FEW FILTHY MOLES!
CALM DOWN NOW, GEORGE. NOBODY'S TAKING ANYTHING AWAY FROM YOU.
THAT'S RIGHT!
THESE MOLES ARE A DIME A DOZEN. I CAN HAVE A WHOLE NEW CREW IN TOWN ON MONDAY.
YOU WANNA CUT WEIGHT? LET'S CUT WEIGHT.
END OF THE LINE. EVERYBODY OFF!
WHAT ARE Y'ALL WAITING FOR?! I SAID GIT!
YOU START HOPPING OR I START SHOOTING!

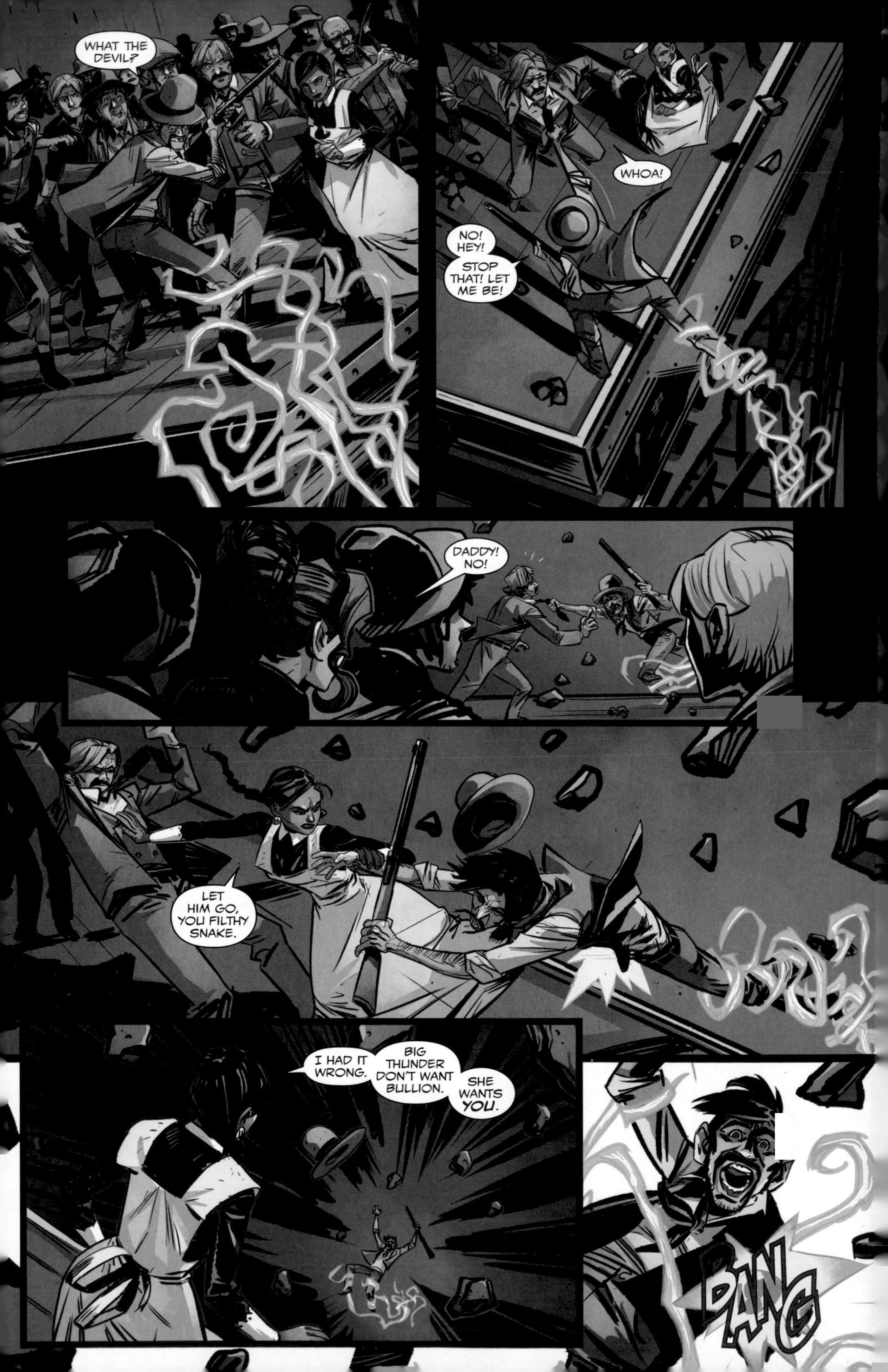

WHAT THE DEVIL?
WHOA!
NO! HEY!
STOP THAT! LET ME BE!
DADDY! NO!
LET HIM GO, YOU FILTHY SNAKE.
I HAD IT WRONG.
BIG THUNDER DON'T WANT BULLION.
SHE WANTS YOU.
BANG

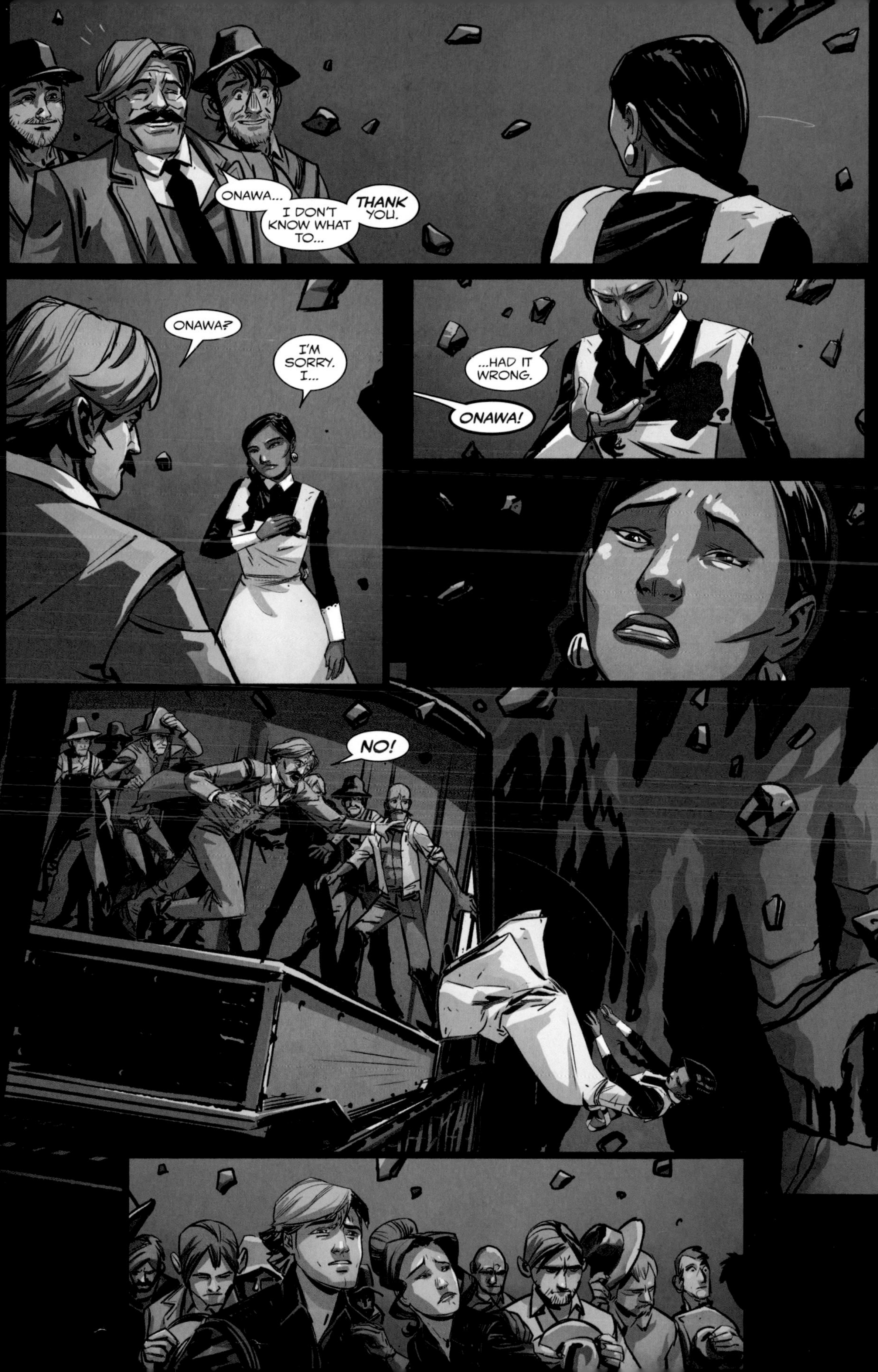
ONAWA... I DON'T KNOW WHAT TO...
THANK YOU.
ONAWA?
I'M SORRY. I...
...HAD IT WRONG.
ONAWA!
NO!

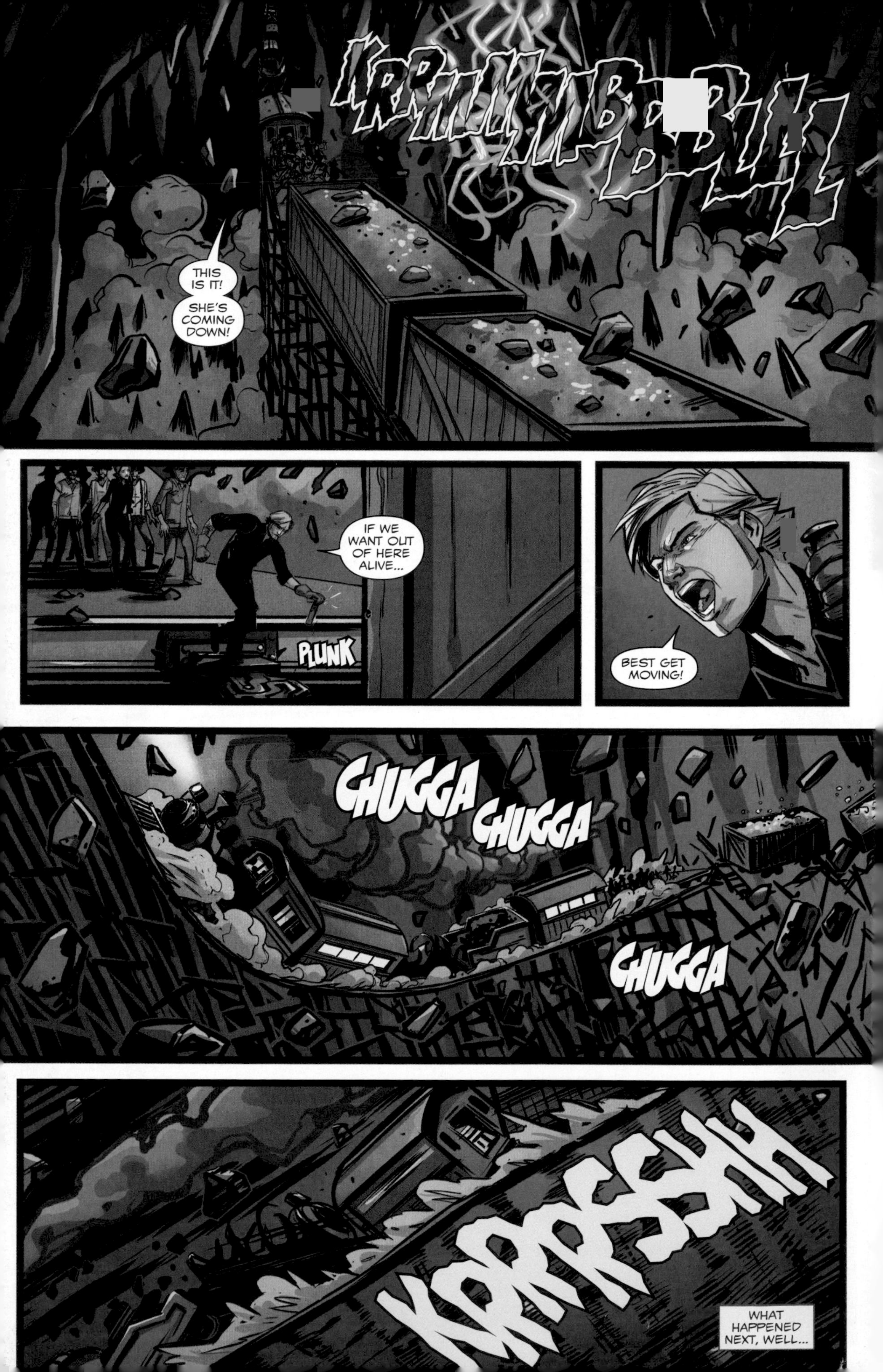

THIS IS IT!
SHE'S COMING DOWN!
IF WE WANT OUT OF HERE ALIVE...
PLUNK
BEST GET MOVING!
CHUGGA
CHUGGA
CHUGGA
WHAT HAPPENED NEXT, WELL...

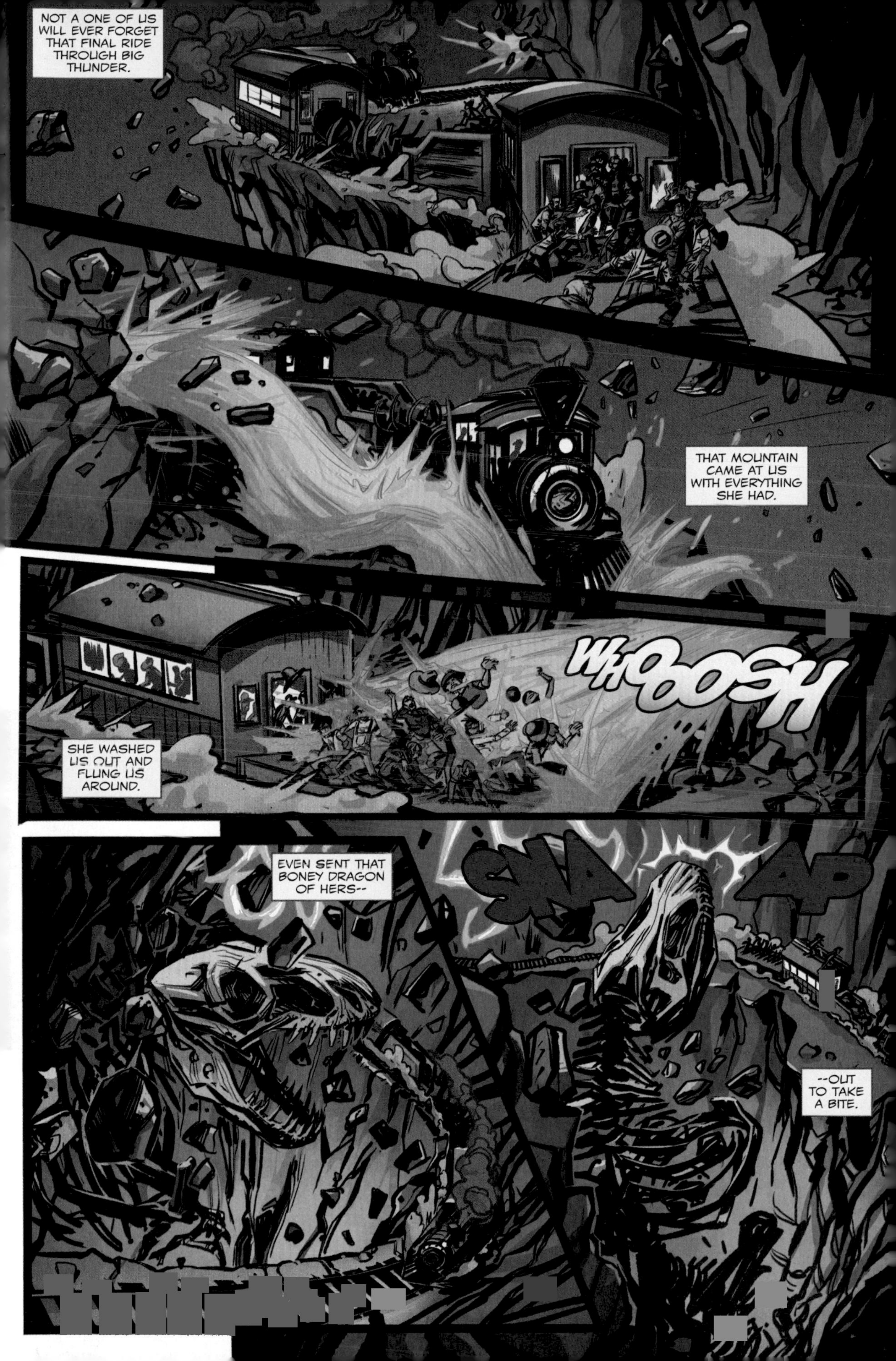
NOT A ONE OF US WILL EVER FORGET THAT FINAL RIDE THROUGH BIG THUNDER.
THAT MOUNTAIN CAME AT US WITH EVERYTHING SHE HAD.
WHOOSH
SHE WASHED US OUT AND FLUNG US AROUND.
EVEN SENT THAT BONEY DRAGON OF HERS--
SNAAP
--OUT TO TAKE A BITE.

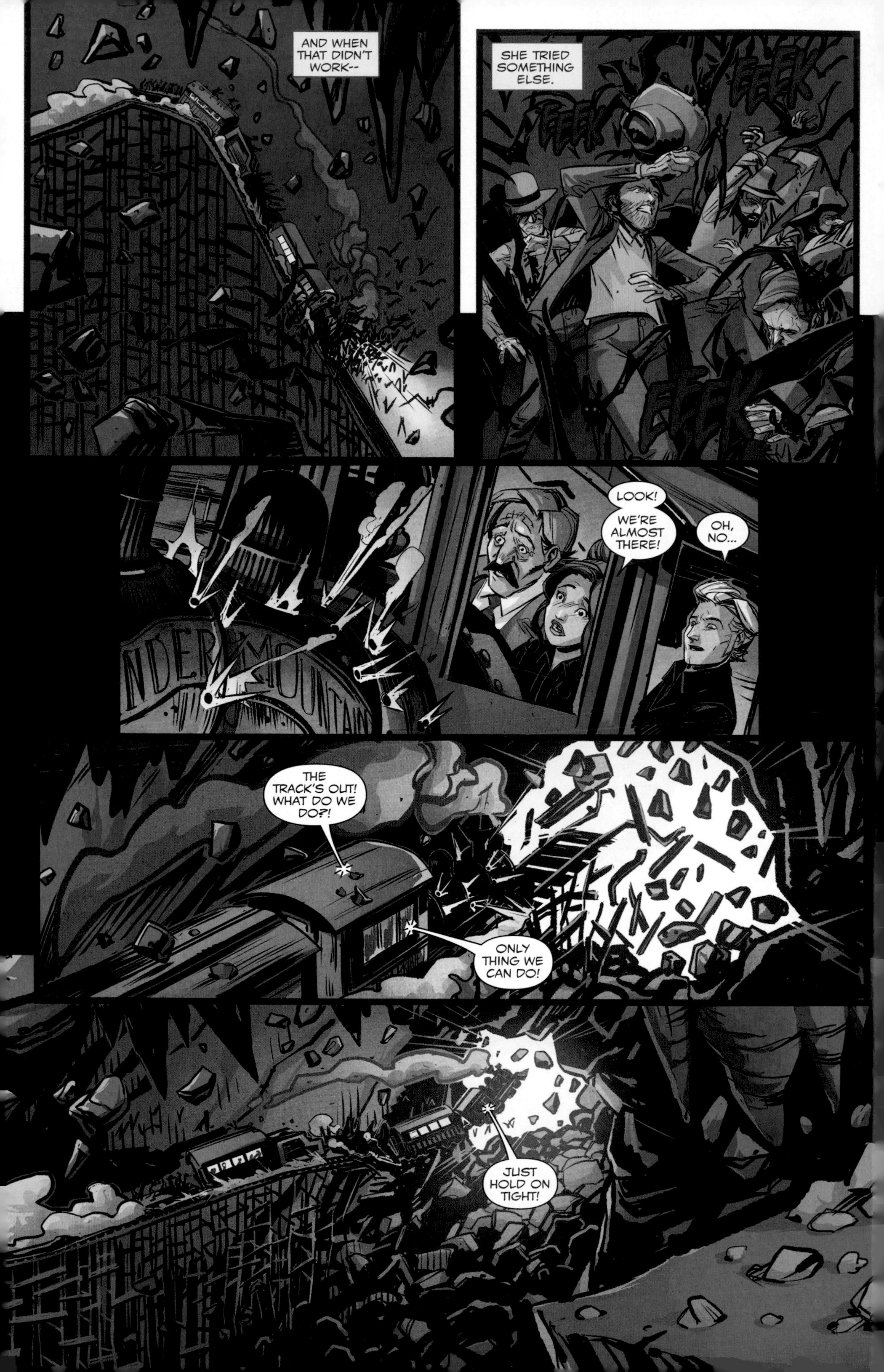
AND WHEN THAT DIDN'T WORK--
SHE TRIED SOMETHING ELSE.
EEEEK
EEEEK
EEEEK
EEEK
LOOK!
WE'RE ALMOST THERE!
OH, NO...
THE TRACK'S OUT! WHAT DO WE DO?!
ONLY THING WE CAN DO!
JUST HOLD ON TIGHT!

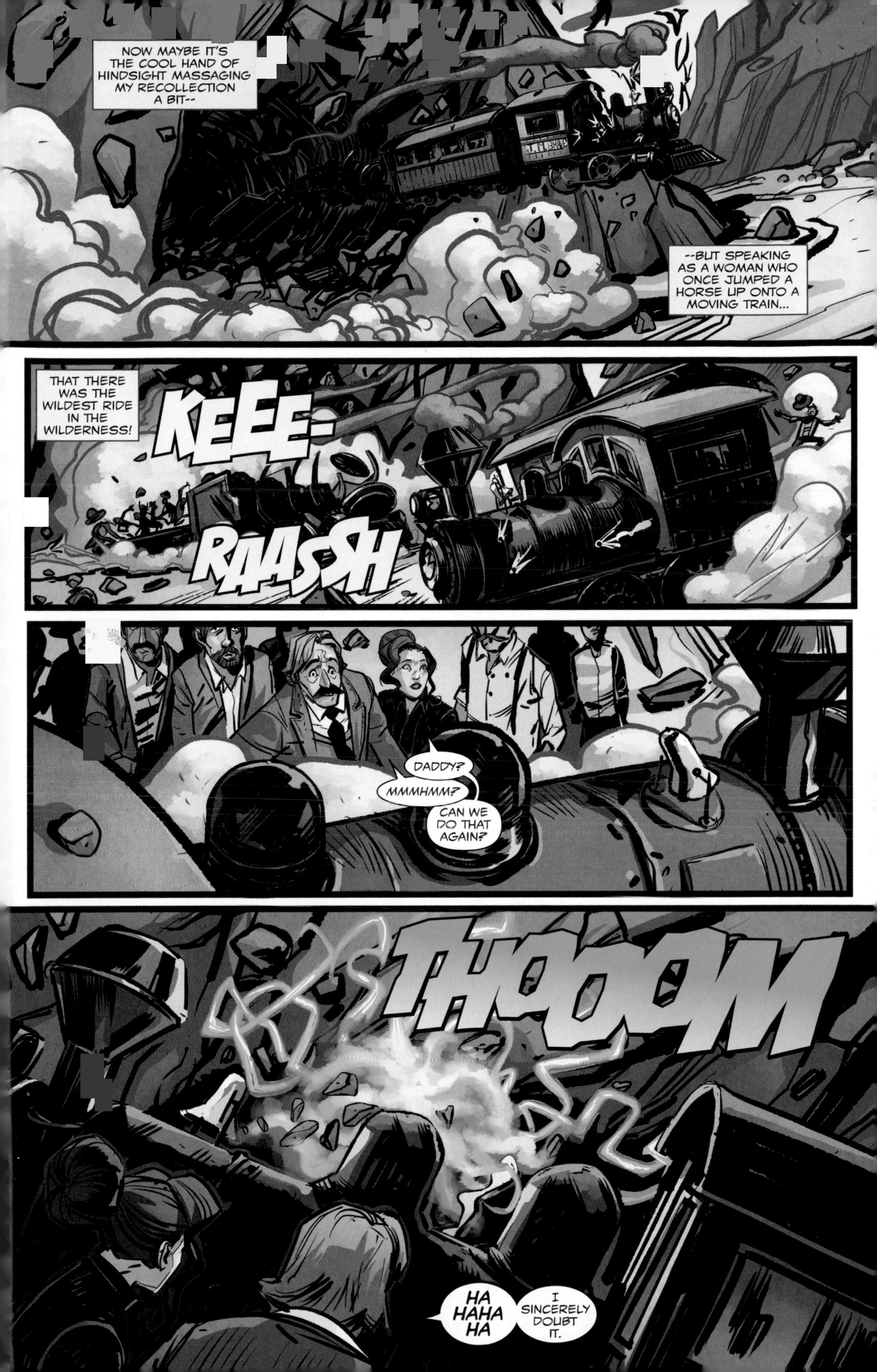
NOW MAYBE IT'S THE COOL HAND OF HINDSIGHT MASSAGING MY RECOLLECTION A BIT--
--BUT SPEAKING AS A WOMAN WHO ONCE JUMPED A HORSE UP ONTO A MOVING TRAIN...
THAT THERE WAS THE WILDEST RIDE IN THE WILDERNESS!
KEEE-
RAASSH
DADDY?
MMMHMM?
CAN WE DO THAT AGAIN?
THOOOM
HA HAHA HA
I SINCERELY DOUBT IT.

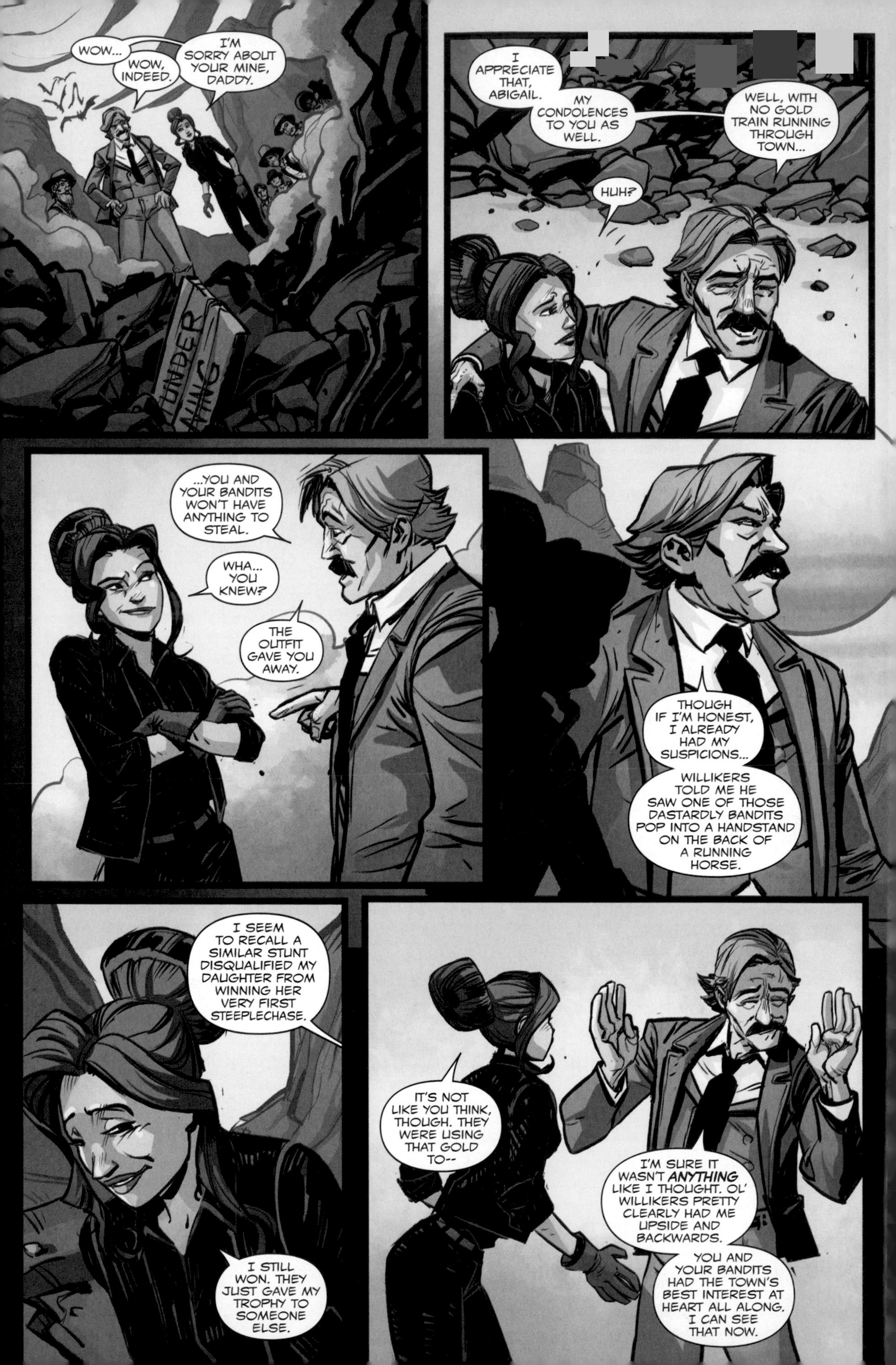
WOW...
WOW, INDEED.
I'M SORRY ABOUT YOUR MINE, DADDY.
UNDER
I APPRECIATE THAT, ABIGAIL.
MY CONDOLENCES TO YOU AS WELL.
WELL, WITH NO GOLD TRAIN RUNNING THROUGH TOWN...
HUH?
...YOU AND YOUR BANDITS WON'T HAVE ANYTHING TO STEAL.
WHA... YOU KNEW?
THE OUTFIT GAVE YOU AWAY.
THOUGH IF I'M HONEST, I ALREADY HAD MY SUSPICIONS...
WILLIKERS TOLD ME HE SAW ONE OF THOSE DASTARDLY BANDITS POP INTO A HANDSTAND ON THE BACK OF A RUNNING HORSE.
I SEEM TO RECALL A SIMILAR STUNT DISQUALIFIED MY DAUGHTER FROM WINNING HER VERY FIRST STEEPLECHASE.
I STILL WON. THEY JUST GAVE MY TROPHY TO SOMEONE ELSE.
IT'S NOT LIKE YOU THINK, THOUGH. THEY WERE USING THAT GOLD TO--
I'M SURE IT WASN'T **ANYTHING** LIKE I THOUGHT. OL' WILLIKERS PRETTY CLEARLY HAD ME UPSIDE AND BACKWARDS.
YOU AND YOUR BANDITS HAD THE TOWN'S BEST INTEREST AT HEART ALL ALONG. I CAN SEE THAT NOW.

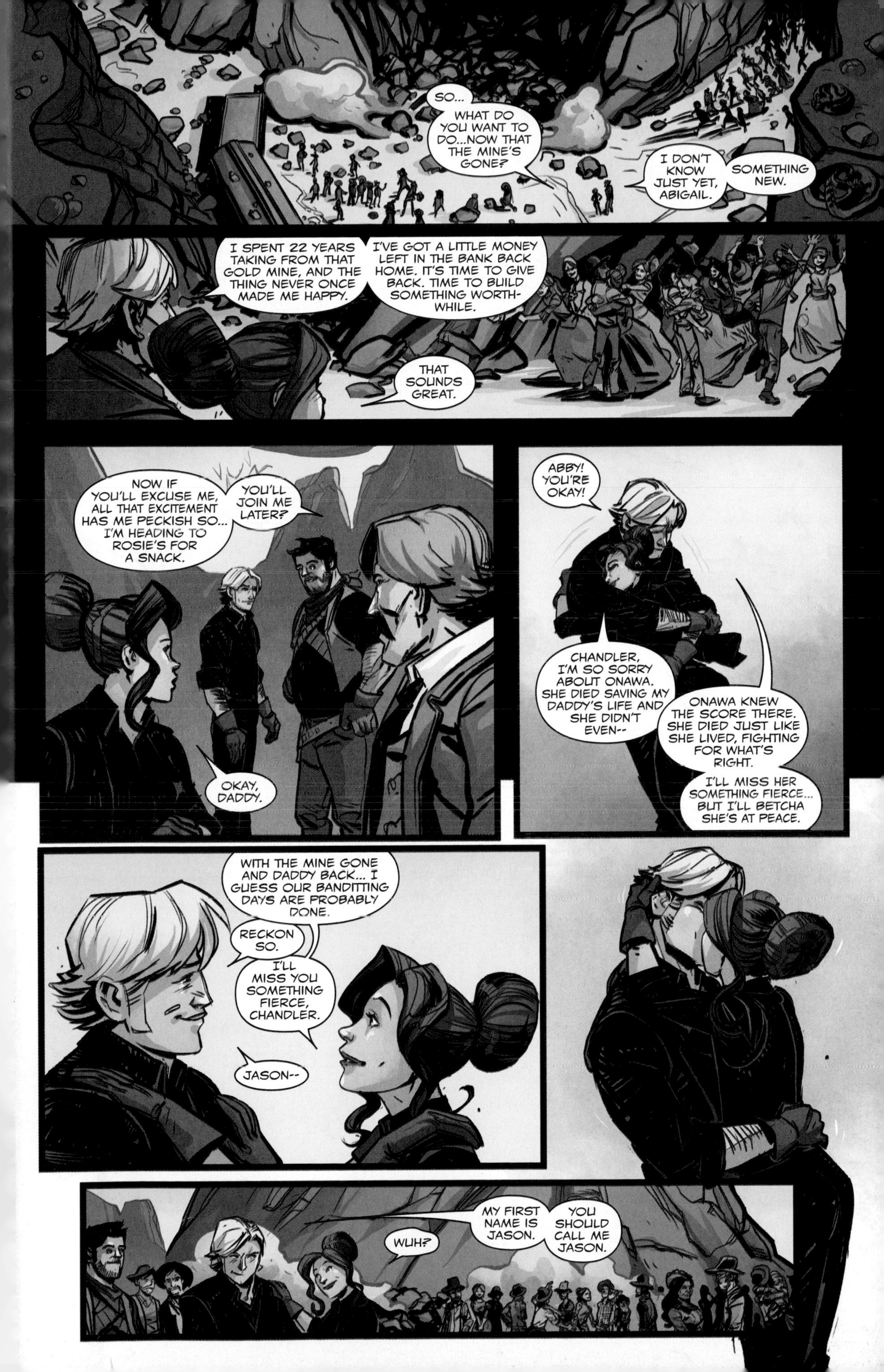
SO...
WHAT DO YOU WANT TO DO...NOW THAT THE MINE'S GONE?
I DON'T KNOW JUST YET, ABIGAIL.
SOMETHING NEW.
I SPENT 22 YEARS TAKING FROM THAT GOLD MINE, AND THE THING NEVER ONCE MADE ME HAPPY.
I'VE GOT A LITTLE MONEY LEFT IN THE BANK BACK HOME. IT'S TIME TO GIVE BACK. TIME TO BUILD SOMETHING WORTH-WHILE.
THAT SOUNDS GREAT.
NOW IF YOU'LL EXCUSE ME, ALL THAT EXCITEMENT HAS ME PECKISH SO... I'M HEADING TO ROSIE'S FOR A SNACK.
YOU'LL JOIN ME LATER?
OKAY, DADDY.
ABBY! YOU'RE OKAY!
CHANDLER, I'M SO SORRY ABOUT ONAWA. SHE DIED SAVING MY DADDY'S LIFE AND SHE DIDN'T EVEN--
ONAWA KNEW THE SCORE THERE. SHE DIED JUST LIKE SHE LIVED, FIGHTING FOR WHAT'S RIGHT.
I'LL MISS HER SOMETHING FIERCE... BUT I'LL BETCHA SHE'S AT PEACE.
WITH THE MINE GONE AND DADDY BACK... I GUESS OUR BANDITTING DAYS ARE PROBABLY DONE.
RECKON SO.
I'LL MISS YOU SOMETHING FIERCE, CHANDLER.
JASON--
WUH?
MY FIRST NAME IS JASON.
YOU SHOULD CALL ME JASON.

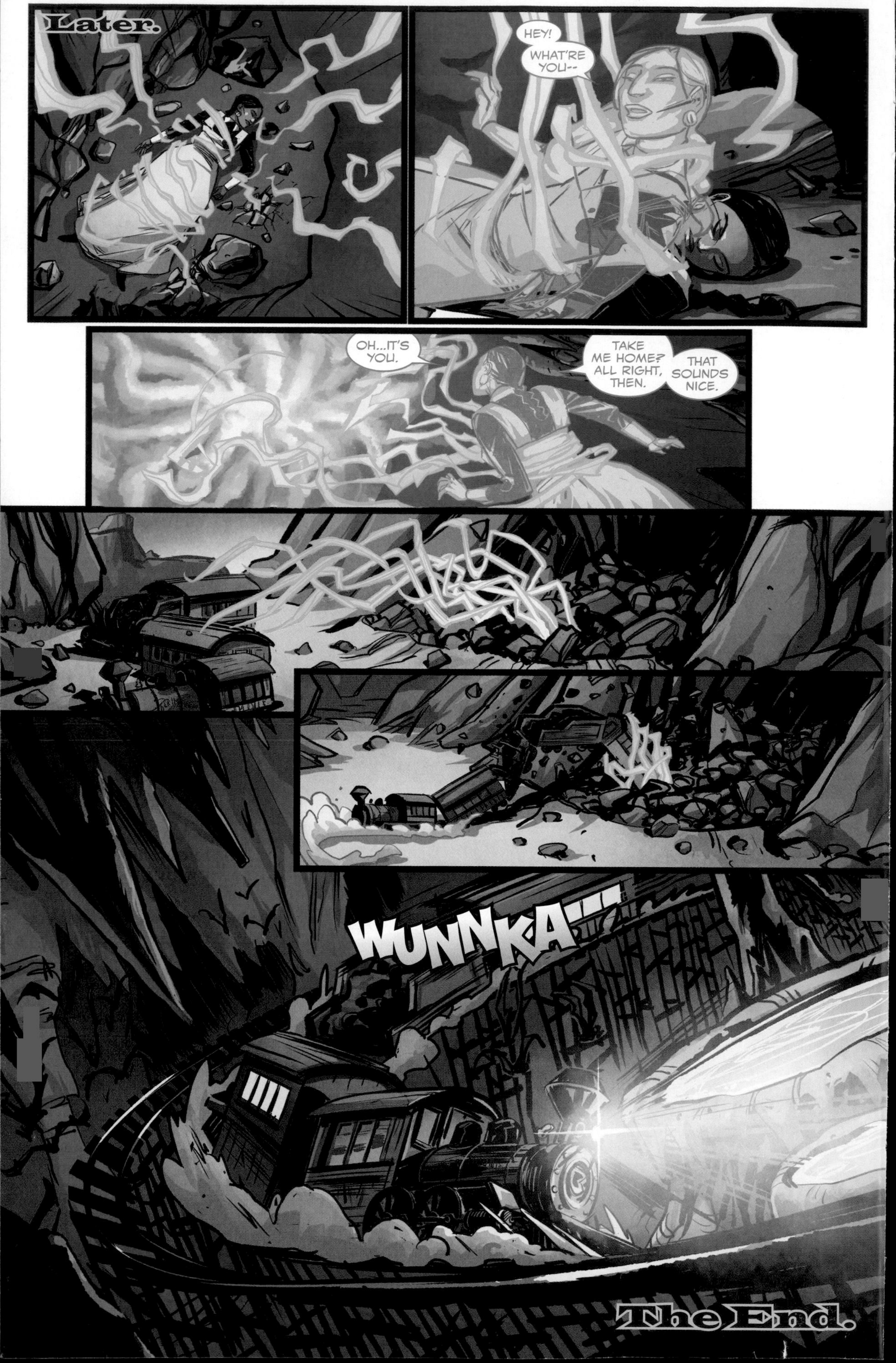
Later.
HEY!
WHAT'RE YOU--
OH...IT'S YOU.
TAKE ME HOME? ALL RIGHT, THEN.
THAT SOUNDS NICE.
WUNNKA!!!
The End.